"Every man must choose."

BECOME WANTED ENTERTAINMENT
PRESENTS

ACT TWO

A Story Created by
DAVID GEARY

Editor and Writer
CESAR HINOJOSA

Executive Writer
DAVID GEARY

Copyright © 2018 by

BECOME WANTED ENTERTAINMENT

Printed and Bound in the United States of America

All characters appearing in this work are fictitious.
Any resemblance to real persons, living or dead, is purely coincidental.

ISBN: 978-0-692-04429-2

Original cover art: Michael Penn
All artwork including photography, cover art, and the Become Wanted logo Copyright © 2018 by
BECOME WANTED ENTERTAINMENT

BECOME WANTED ENTERTAINMENT
Second Printing
www.becomewanted.com

ARTS & LETTERS

BECOME WANTED: ACT TWO

Fantastic fans and readers,

I was recently commissioned to create a cover illustration for the action-packed crime story, *Become Wanted*. I was also tasked to create the hero of the series in a style that was different from what I am known for.

Conversely, I do enjoy a great challenge, and I quickly developed an appreciation for the creator's faith that I could pull it off.

I began to draw inspiration from that of a 1940's noir comic strip, the incredible likeness of well-known cover artists, and BOOM! I was on my way.

I hope our readers and fans of the series will enjoy the art as much as I enjoyed creating it. The journey was a great one.

All the best to this team, and again, thank you for the chance to be a part of this awesome project!

Mike Penn

GOOD MORNING FREELAND

BECOME WANTED: ACT TWO

As the sun rises over the horizon, it casts a warm golden glow across the sprawling cityscape, signaling the beginning of a new day. The citizens of the magnificent metropolis begin to stir, their energy renewed, and their spirits lifted by the promise of another day's potential.

In the heart of the bustling city, honking horns and revving engines grow louder as the morning rush hour traffic picks up. The hum of activity is punctuated by the clanging and banging of metal on metal as the construction crew assembles at the foot of a towering, unfinished skyscraper.

*"Hello! I am **Skyland's Finest**-Susan Winters, and join me for 'Good Morning Freeland!' Our city is booming, and I am thrilled to report that the new Homecoming building is nearly complete and set to finish by the end of this month. It's truly a massive structure and an accurate testament to Freeland's improvement.*

GOOD MORNING FREELAND

DING!

Achieving the top level at Skyland News Headquarters, a silver set of elevator doors chime open, and a familiar woman in stern heels marches out. Leading into what sounds like incoherent shouting, she barges through the branch's glass access with tremendous frustration.

"This shit is ridiculous." In the newsroom, phones are ringing, television monitors are buzzing, and Skyland clerks rush to distribute work files within the earsplitting department. "You're not going to get a better story than this."

"Um…Susan, you can't go in there!"

"Shut up, Larry!"

"Shit."

Seeking no one's approval, she locates the door nob and bursts into an office to find the Editor-in-Chief of Skyland News resting casually in the company's chair.

BECOME WANTED: ACT TWO

"YOU'RE FLOATING MY STORY, DENNIS?" Dennis, a rather patient man, appears unbothered as if he were waiting for her to find him with more than just a friendly request. "Well, Dennis?" His silver fox hair and goatee give him away, not to mention his exceeding belly and thin reading glasses resting on his twisted nose, as presented in all of his famous photographs.

Finally, the executive inhales deeply in preparation for another confrontation with his best journalist. Despite his reputation for being overbearing and stubborn, he is as lenient as one can be regarding Susan. However, today is not one of those days.

"What'd you expect?" he retorts. The old-timer's response baffles the journalist, forcing her to take a brief time-out.

"I find it funny that you'd send me back to Harlot's just for you to pull it from underneath my feet!" Having felt betrayed, Susan pokes her director with a warm notice, starting with her index finger pinned to a familiar report placed at the edge of his desk, "And I hope you're not expecting me to re-write it!" Suddenly, with his thoughts collected, the news director leans forward with his hands firmly folded.

"Nonsense, Susan. I don't expect you to rewrite it. Just get me that follow-up on the Harlot's situation, will you?" He begs.

"And if I don't?"

"Close the door." The two share a short recess, and eventually, Susan snags the office's only entry with her heel and kicks it shut. Meantime, Dennis rests his papers to remove his glasses. "Our ratings are shooting through the roof, we've got city officials backing us, and hell, who doesn't admire your dexterity? "If it weren't for your grand ambition, this station would be in a shitty rut!"

"What does this all have to do with my report?"

"Real crime sells, young lady—not some

urban speculation!"

"Speculation? Since when has my work ever been 'speculation,' Dennis?"

"Never! Which is why I'm pulling your story. We've got robbers from last week still on the loose, yet you want to waste this studio's time on some mysterious doctor."

"He's real, Dennis!"

"He is a myth, Susan! And this—" he grabs her report, "This will backfire, not only on you but Skyland, too."

"You don't know that."

"Yes, I do, dammit!" he shouts. "Ever since that dumpster incident near JJ's, you tried to convince me and this entire station that all these masked terrorists are somehow associated with one another, and I'm not buying it, Susan," he says. "We're not here to write comic books!"

"Don't patronize me," she says, and while the entire news team witnesses their exchange through the blinds, Dennis takes notice.

GOOD MORNING FREELAND

"Alright, that's enough." Reaching his limit, Dennis takes to his feet to teach the journalist a thing or two about capturing great stories. "I'll hand it to you. You're willing to fight tooth and nail for what you believe to be the best article to ever land on my desk." Next, he lifts his right hand to present three chubby fingers, "But until you learn to follow Skyland's three crucial steps, you won't have one worth following." he finishes.

"C'mon, Dennis…really?"

"Just stick to the grieving war hero for now, is that understood?"

"Sure, I'll get on that right away!"

Dennis watches Susan storm out, feeling a twinge of guilt for dismissing her. However, he firmly believes that sticking to Skyland's proven formula is the key, and with a deep sigh, he returns to the task at hand, silently hoping that she will understand the importance of fitting within the station's established framework.

A GODFATHER'S CONCERN

A GODFATHER'S CONCERN

The roaring GTO arrives at Freeland's incredible police station, where the city's heroes operate and where the late Michael Gibson became the great detective.

Achieving the parking line near the front entrance, the courageous Marcus Gibson steps out of his vehicle to find police officers patrolling the foundation among an arrangement of brave sedans remaining just outside. It has been nearly a decade since he'd last visited the place of his father's work. Nonetheless, he dons his signature sunglasses, closes the door behind him, and proceeds to enter the precinct.

Passing through a set of wood-framed double doors, he immediately takes a wall as a stampede pushes through the vestibule when one recognizes him from JJ's Tavern.

"Hey, it's great to see you again, soldier!" Marcus nods before moving on.

Entering the foyer supplied with wooden benches and an unattended check-in desk with a notepad and pencil, Marcus quickly discovers that much has changed since he last remembered, not to mention his father's absence.

Examining the standard area, he detects the crystallized interior windows and multiple bulletin boards posted along the nearby walls when a familiar voice seizes his attention.

"STAY DOWN!"

Curious to see the fuss, Marcus sneaks to the bend and peeks in to uncover an active crowd cheering on a brave policeman while a valiant battle shield and combat baton rest on a vacant countertop.

Nonetheless, Marcus remains confident, believing the outcome will lean in favor of his graceless friend.

"ARGH! FUCK OFF, COP!"

Besting the crook, the capable cop forms a chop-hand and strikes him upon his throat, followed by a stern push-kick to send him away.

A GODFATHER'S CONCERN

Now furious, the policeman sounds off and goes in for a unique take-down, slamming the outsized threat on the deck for good.

WHAM!

"See! Totally unnecessary!"

Suddenly, the foyer applauds and celebrates who turns out to be none other than Officer Brian Bronson.

"Oh, this is entertaining for you, huh?" Exhausted, Bronson eventually locates his spotless glass shield for defense and bends an elbow to steal a breath.

"You're hard to break, Brian." The handsome policeman grins.

"Welcome to headquarters," he motions strongly, sitting on the menacing crook.

"Is that your *Bulldog*?"

"Who? Him? Nah. Ironically, we did fish out the real mutt last night," Marcus' smile gradually disappears as Bronson continues, "Yeah! We pulled him from the river at the docks along with two others, and it wasn't the water that killed them, I'll tell you that."

"Hey, you're that war hero…thank you for your service, man," mutters the offender.

"See! Even the bad guys love you," the comedic policeman says, "So. You here to see the Commissioner?"

"Yes; where do I go from here?"

"Straight ahead, and next time, bring me a coffee will ya."

Entering the precinct's threshold, Marcus finds a much older constable sitting at the reception desk, filling out paperwork.

"Still checking for grammar and punctuation, Mr. Hamilton?" Officer Hamilton, the precinct's seasoned operative, looks up, squinting his eyes tightly behind his reading specs.

"M-Marcus? Marcus, my boy!" he blurts. Officer Hamilton is an overset man, short compared to Marcus, but fully capable of defending himself with a pair of old mitts. "Lord, you've grown to be tall and tough!"

A GODFATHER'S CONCERN

Aside from his appearance, he is aging wonderfully, with a head full of white hair and a thick Walrus mustache. Additionally, he obtains the longest employee record in the precinct, surpassing the Commissioner, which gives him tenure over many in the station.

"It's truly been a while, Mr. Hamilton." Reaching out to shake his hand, the kind constable receives the gesture and pulls the war hero close to embrace him, "Just call me Bill, Marcus." he insists. "Now, let me show you around the old thing."

"Right behind you, Bill."

Moments in, the two enter the outrageous bullpen, where they discover several divisions collaborating to further their impressive investigations within an octagon-shaped command desk.

"Here is where the important work takes place." Numerous agents working on their cases stop to acknowledge them briefly and continue to file away. "They're a sharp bunch, but your father could outsmart them all."

"Attention to detail is very important, Bill."

"Absolutely. I'm sure you found your friend, Brian, horsing around back at booking. It's where all the paperwork gets done after an arrest."

"Oh, yeah; Officer Bronson is a rowdy one."

"Watch that one; his fancy for whiskey will do him more bad than good someday." Bill's sheer honesty motions Marcus to pull the next door for him. He remembers a different Brian growing up. However, things change when you're gone that long. "And here we are.

"Well, until we meet again, Mr. Hamilton.

"Bill, Marcus."

"Right."

"It was Sherman's idea to take the distant department in the building. Our Chief Bluecoat lives up to his name and is a very busy policeman." Nearing the office, Bill turns to Marcus with one last notion, "Go easy on the big guy. He cared for your father more than he was allowed to, and I'm sure he's doing everything in his power to catch the bastard behind it."

"Give me a moment, Bill!"

"Thank you for the tour."

"My pleasure. It was good to see you, my boy."

Marcus enters to find the Commissioner on an urgent phone call. Yet, Sherman gestures for him to have a seat. Observing his office, he recognizes a display of decorative awards and framed photos hanging on the walls, including a photograph of Sherman and Marcus' late father, Michael. Conclusively, the Commissioner hangs up the phone.

"Geez, I'm sorry about that. It's good to see you again," Sherman gestures to a seat, "Did my guys treat you well out there?"

"They did."

"And how about that Bronson?"

BECOME WANTED: ACT TWO

"You know, Brian. Can't keep that guy down."

"That's funny. So, what reasons brought you here today?"

"My father and your friend."

"Fair enough. It's been damn near a month, and we still have nothing. Things have become problematic with your father gone, and many theorize that his death unleashed new sorts of threats, and we still don't have any updates on your masked maniac, only more bodies from the situation at Harlot's." Drilled in discipline, the clever soldier remains silent on the matter, concealing his involvement that night nonetheless. "Listen, son. I got good guys out there tackling crime, and no man's life is worth someone's evil deeds," he speaks. Meanwhile, Sherman brings his hands together with a keen stare directed at Marcus, "Which is why I need you to stay out of the way."

"I beg your pardon?"

A GODFATHER'S CONCERN

"Thanks to Skyland and their precious asset, Susan Winters, they've caught wind of your presence. Therefore, I strongly suggest you lay low before something ugly happens."

"I can't do that." The valiant soldier's steep determination catches Commissioner Sherman off guard. Thus, he draws on the memory of the war hero's late father to further drive his point.

"You possess his resolve, but Freeland is at war," he explains. "Things become personal here, Marcus, and I refuse to preside over your funeral if things were to spill over." As the pressure between them thickens, Sherman's phone interrupts, summoning their attention.

RING, RING!

"Let me take this," he states. Marcus is sealed behind a wall. Even with the secret billfold in his possession, he won't make it far without Sherman's backing.

"Sure." Respecting the Commissioner's need for privacy, Marcus rises to his feet and

BECOME WANTED: ACT TWO

seeks a discreet exit when Sherman—

"Wait, son."

"Sir?"

"I want to thank you for your service to this nation. You've done more than enough. Now, allow us to handle the rest."

RING, RIIING!

The endless ringing grates on Marcus's nerves, provoking him to slip away as the Commissioner finally answers the call.

Strolling the vacant passageway with the precinct's historical battle shield fastened to his arm, Brian connects with Marcus in passing, supposing he and the Commissioner's discussion didn't go over well.

"Still bringing me that coffee?" he asks. Rather dejectedly, Marcus simply renders a thumbs-up and finds his way out. "Shit...what did you say this time?" he mutters. But then—

"Bronson! Get in here!" Sherman shouts, summoning the nervy policeman to return the glass defense where it belongs.

A GODFATHER'S CONCERN

"Not a scratch on it," Brian jeers. He and Sherman have a unique relationship, whereas Bronson often teases the Commissioner by knowing just how far he can push any given envelope on a good day.

"Stop toying with your old man's things," says Sherman. What was once his highfather's unbreakable shield now wins its place in the Commissioner's ward as a remembrance of Freeland's sole protectors. "Do you know why he entrusted me with that, Brian?" he asks.

"To spare me the pressure of carrying his legacy, sir," he finishes.

"Very good," he says. Yet, weary of his Godson's next measures, he gathers his beliefs and awards his most trusted with a very tricky assignment. "Keep a close watch on Marcus, and uh…take my car."

Sensing something amiss, Brian moves to the door, dabbing the antique on his way out.

"10-4."

ABSTRACT

Freeland's citizens have come to count on Commissioner Ronald P. Sherman's incredible insight, diplomatic measures, and steadfast charge against Freeland's crime. He's seen the city fall once before, but not on his watch. For twenty years, Commissioner Sherman has maintained law and order in his town, thus earning him a mighty reputation of unparalleled caliber and an indispensable asset to the community.

EXTRA

The Commissioner's path has been a challenging one. He has witnessed many of Freeland's most spirited heroes fall. Likewise, he has clashed with the city's most dangerous crooks, including Danny Black, Mayek Breaker, and even the Red Gate ninja clan.

WARRANT

Welcome to Freeland City, where fearless crime fighters rise to become legends, incredible crooks become infamous threats, and the clinically unhinged become dangerously unstoppable.

Become Wanted

ANOTHER LEAD

ANOTHER LEAD

As the sun sets, Marcus enters the gates of the Police Memorial in the GTO. He's been busy and, perhaps, too busy to catch up with Freeland City's great loss. Clearing the key, Marcus takes a moment to collect his thoughts and exits his vehicle.

With each step he takes, light gusts of wind begin to drive against him, adding to his sorrow. Nonetheless, he travels onward.

Finally, he arrives at the great detective's gravestone. Despite his usual strength, he's stuck, overwhelmed by the uncertainty of that moment when his father, Michael, was murdered.

"How did you not see your killer coming? You was the best detective this city ever knew."

The question has haunted Marcus since. Therefore, he must pursue this path, and the billfold may contain the riddle behind his father's death.

\#

BECOME WANTED: ACT TWO

Isolated at JJ's Tavern, a solitary ceiling fan whirrs above a brooding police officer perched at the bar. The scene surrounding him is calm, yet his heart is loaded with unspoken emotions as tension simmers just beneath the surface.

"What's troubling you, Brian?" Ever the empathetic ear, the barkeeper leans in with a brow furrowed with concern.

"Marcus," he replies, stretched with the weight of his worry. "I can't shake the feeling that he's hurting more than he lets on, you know?" As he delves into memories of their youth, Brian's eyes grow distant and clouded with sadness. "We were inseparable, dreaming of becoming heroes, and we did; he enlisted, and I wore the badge," he reveals. "I kept our streets safe, while he fought in wars that leave men broken; and his father...man, his father was his hero. He was *our* hero, and now...he's gone."

Aiming to ease the weight on Bronson's

shoulders, JJ returns with a relaxing gesture in the form of a—

"Here…this one's on me." To Brian's surprise, a tall, amber-filled glass appears before him as a small token of solace from the bartender. "That'll be your last one for the night, kid." Therefore, Brian continues.

"I want to help him…but I'm at a loss," he confesses. Refusing his worries to break him, Brian downs the drink and pushes away from the bar, leaving behind a few crumpled bills as the liquid fire ignites his determination. "Thanks, Jerry."

Racing under an evening's moonbeam, Brian reaches for the driver's side, slides in behind the steering wheel, and ignites Sherman's old police sedan. As it roars to life, he pulls away from the tavern, determined to save his friend from an unforeseen danger that awaits.

#

BECOME WANTED: ACT TWO

As the evening newscast comes to an end, the news floor erupts with activity while the crew labors diligently to prepare the set for the next program, and as for Susan Winters, she quietly slips away from the anchor's desk, feeling somewhat blue.

Since her clash with Dennis earlier, she couldn't shake off the disappointment that her story about the bizarre doctor didn't make it to the evening broadcast. As of no wonder to her, Skyland is widely observed for featuring dramatic tales of heroes and intense police politics, whereas the subtle peculiarities lurking underneath Freeland's surface are rarely delved into.

Striding past Sales, Programming, and Business, Susan eventually retreats to her safe space illuminated by mild, ambient lighting. The walls are decked with awards and framed newspaper articles, each highlighting her past achievements and the high standards she has set for herself.

ANOTHER LEAD

Taking center stage, a sleek wooden desk with journalism reference materials stacked atop bids her a warm welcome.

"I missed you, too," she adds. Determined to refine her story, Susan settles into her chair, not before noticing a small framed photo of her and Michael positioned at the corner of her workspace. Freeland may have lost their hero, but she has not given up on her promise to the late detective. "C'mon, Marcus...lead me to him."

#

As night falls, the harmonious sound of crickets fills the air outside Marcus' home when suddenly, the GTO's headlights illuminate the curb near the mailbox.

Latching the door behind him, Marcus starts up the stairs and into his study to locate the billfold exposed by the pale moonlight passing through the window.

BECOME WANTED: ACT TWO

"Forgive me, Uncle Sherman."

Meanwhile, as the suspense develops, the fog returns, creeping in from the street. Its phantom presence, although lacking form, hails suspicion all the same.

Rising quicker as the darkness from the sky deepens, the uncanny character, cloaked and caped, finally emerges in time to witness Marcus speed away.

Pursuing him not, he simply remains, weighing the crime fighter's next charge.

"Beware, Marcus… Simon is not to be underestimated."

ANOTHER THREAT

BECOME WANTED: ACT TWO

Beyond Diana's incredible entrance, the scene is alive, well-lit, and wafted with the haze of cigarette smoke hanging in the air. Hop music fills the atmosphere while the gorgeous waitresses, all trimmed in sparkling dresses, weave through the crowd, serving booze and cold starters to the well-dressed patrons. But then, as the night wears on, the scene finally darkens, inviting the entire room to tune in.

FLASH!

Sitting behind a grand piano, a handsome pianist, revealed under a spotlight, prepares his music sheet as the seductive Alma Arcos enters the stage. As she approaches a gleaming vocal microphone, the musician closes his eyes and feels for the keys. Then, as Alma inhales, his fingers begin to dance across the panel with practiced precision, drawing the attention of those watching, and with a slow inhale, Alma begins to sing, her seductive presence filling the room.

ANOTHER THREAT

"Mi corazon duele por ti...Como un trogon en una jaula tratando de ser libre..."

Her devoted voice and gestures are captivating. Thus, earning the eye of one Astor Eckhard. Furthermore, the crowd remains deeply touched as the sophisticated performance unfolds.

"¿Quién puede salvarme de este dolor? ¿Quién puede liberarme de esta jaula?"

#

Arriving in his righteous car, Marcus recognizes a sizeable manufactory beyond the ground's faded sign hanging just above the main entrance that reads: "Phillip's and Son's." Curious, he unravels the file, stashed in his coat pocket, to verify the location and quietly drives in.

Unknowingly, another vehicle, parked nearby and out of sight, rolls in softly behind him.

BECOME WANTED: ACT TWO

#

Back at a familiar residence, Officer Brian Bronson arrives drunk, according to an empty bottle glued to his hand. Feeling for the keys wedged in the sedan's ignition, the sloshed policeman cuts the engine, unbuckles his seatbelt, and wobbles to the front porch.

"Marcus, I'm here for you, pal," he calls. Mustering a lazy index finger, he locates the doorbell to summon the crime fighter, who is unavailable, evidently. "Marcus! Give it up already...the boss wants you to lay low!" Eager to find his friend, Brian attempts to climb through an open window, only to fall into the bushes sprouting around the home. Eventually, he seeks the curb near the mailbox to sober up. "Where did you go?"

Pondering his reasons, misplaced rather, for invading Marcus' property, the odor of motor oil suddenly peaks his attention, following fresh tire tracks beneath his shoes.

ANOTHER THREAT

#

Placing both hands on the twin doorway, Marcus forces them open to reveal the smell of lumber, indicating a wood factory of some sort. The war hero closes the doors behind him, sealing him in from the outside.

#

"Dispatch, come in." A sturdy hand navigates the steering wheel of a police sedan while the other grips the radio receiver hoping for a response.

"This is Central," a female dispatch returns, *"Go ahead, Brian."*

#

Sneaking past various operating stationaries, a sudden gleam from the evening sky reveals Marcus as he navigates the vast lumber mill. However, many signs surrounding the old factory stated that the business closed several years ago. But for the trained soldier, the funk of working grease is a classic giveaway for a practical criminal cover.

#

"Yeah! I'm requesting an update on any incidents reported within the last hour." Climbing the outskirts of Central Freeland, Brian controls the aging car and its rusting parts.

"No disturbances have been reported."

"10-4," he huffs. However, outside his jurisdiction, Officer Bronson focuses on the highway to uncover tall timber and sapwoods leading to "Phillip's and Son's."

#

Infiltrating the finishing area, Marcus

discovers polished circular saws, a high-speed drill board, and his fitted oxfords sinking in sawdust. As he had suspected, men have been working here.

Then, eyeing the only corridor ahead, a nip of dust brushing his bare nostrils brings him down, but with a quick draw of his coat sleeve, he is saved to fight on.

After a brief expedition, Marcus finally reaches the center of the millhouse to discover rows of crates and men in rags assembling, hammering, and loading the nightly inventory.

The operation is at its peak, and posted at the center of the task, high above in the crossbeams, is the factory's wicked operator, monitoring the workforce with his arms criss-crossed firmly behind his spine.

[Quickly! Mr. Eckhard is arriving soon!]

Strangely esteemed among his hirelings, the uncanny Conductor embraces some highly unusual characteristics. He is bald, thin-faced, and gifted with a one-off pair of spectacles. In addition, heavy-duty welding garments cling to his hands and slender frame as a protective measure against lawful intruders. Fixed on gathering answers, Marcus moves forward while crouching to remain out of sight.

[Quickly, men!]

Leaning against a dusty container, he spins around to see a shipping label. Furthermore, curiosity finds Marcus, and as he removes its rustic cover, he discovers items far more significant than he could imagine. But, to his downfall, a sudden sensation tickling his nostrils invokes him to sneeze profoundly.

"A-CHOO!"

[HA! I found you!]

Descending from a glass hatch awning,

ANOTHER THREAT

she drops down without a sound. Her hair, revealed by the moonlight, gives her away. She sneaks beyond standing appliances and through a familiar corridor, where a disturbance stirs her curiosity.

[I have more workers than you have fists!]

  "He's too fast!"
Besting their mallets with his bare hands, Marcus battles through an array of hoods, putting them away as quickly as they come. Meanwhile, the Conductor observes sharply.

[Tired yet?]

  Alas, two goons, worthy of a pounding, are left to stand against the crime fighter, with one surrendered at the collar in his grasp.
  "You first." "No! You first!"

[You halfwits!]

BECOME WANTED: ACT TWO

Next, a sporadic noise amid combat alerts them, including the Conductor. Nonetheless, the two workers drop their hammers and flee, leaving the third to fend against Marcus.

"P-P-Please! Don't hit me!" Next, from the corner of Marcus' view, the artful Susan Winters carefully rises from her hiding position with her clicking tape recorder in hand.

"Hi…"

"Susan?" Shocked to see her, Marcus releases the boy to seek safety. Shifting his focus, he scans the rafters to find the command tower abandoned.

"Where did he go?" Then, in a blink of an eye, the slithering Conductor exposes himself with a dagger in his hand.

"MARCUS, BEHIND YOU!"

WHOOSH!

Frightened, the clumsy reporter stumbles into a stack of crates, leaving the crime fighter with the facility's crooked administrator.

WHOOSH!

ANOTHER THREAT

Leading with his death-dealing bayonet, the Conductor swipes at Marcus relentlessly, forcing him to seek new ground.

"YOU WILL NOT LEAVE THIS FACTORY!"

Following the action from afar, Susan climbs a damaged container and discovers an assortment of assault rifles buried under newspaper and hay.

Realizing her biggest story yet, she tucks her skirt, spins around, and gives her recorder a tremendous whack before pressing play.

WHOOSH!

Evading the screeching villain, Marcus deflects the Conductor's calculated attacks until they ultimately lock wrists.

"Your fighting skills are exceptional," he mentions while catching his breath, "What precinct do you belong to?"

BECOME WANTED: ACT TWO

"Brian, this is dispatch."

"This is Officer Bronson…go ahead."

"There is a robbery in progress. Suspect is male, mean, and dangerous. Think you can take him?"

"Shit…10-4." Then, with a mighty twist of the steering wheel, he spins his vehicle around, and speeds onward.

#

"After all of my years, I have never failed Astor, for I am his most reliable, and once I am finished scattering your body parts across Freeland, he will reward me generously."

Split between Susan and the Conductor, Marcus pulls from deep within and shoves his knee into the villain's gut, followed by a strong push-kick, blasting him into a row of crates.

"I know who you are, Simon Blackwood," he states as the villain crawls back to his feet.

ANOTHER THREAT

"Who are you exactly?" Simon utters.

"Your downfall."

"HA! You ridiculous crime fighter! You are ill-equipped with your fancy punches. You have no idea the reach my employer has. But, by sunrise, your body will be discovered, hanging from a shiny fish hook in East Freeland."

"Talking won't save you from this good ol' beating." Marcus replies.

Unable to intimidate the crime fighter, Simon's threats begin to plummet, and in a blind rage, he jolts from his splinters.

"I will slay you and the reporter next!" Meanwhile, the soldier slides his back leg further to the rear, anchoring his heel in place.

"Not gonna happen." His sights are set, and as Simon nears, Marcus launches a heroic uppercut to defeat the villain once and for all.

WHAM!

Finally, the wretched Conductor is finished, and Marcus lives to see another day.

BECOME WANTED: ACT TWO

"WHAT ARE YOU DOING HERE?"

Steering his outrage with a stern finger, the hero moves in with the journalist fixed on target. "This place is not safe." And as for Susan, however—

"THAT WAS SPECTACULAR!"

Utterly amazed, Susan cuts her recorder and bolts up to clear her skirt of wood chips and sawdust. "This story is going to blow Dennis away!"

"Stay out of my way, Susan."

"And if I don't?"

"All this for another story, huh?" he asks, and still, the gutsy reporter plants her heels, inclined to pursue the crime fighter into even more danger.

"Yes," she confirms.

"Okay."

"Just okay?"

#

ANOTHER THREAT

Surrounded by glasses of fine whiskey and cigar smoke, Alma's ongoing set entrances Astor, drawing his mind away from his affairs.

Then, a mysterious messenger, keenly attired in fancy fabrics unavailable to many, emerges with urgent particulars surrounding the brute's area of operation. Hence, Astor's henchmen lend their attention with their fists equipped and ready.

"There's a problem," he says. The messenger quickly inspects the room around them to ensure no one is listening in. "The shipment has been compromised, and the cops are en route. Fix it quickly, Mr. Eckhard."

Upon receiving this news, Astor's expression hardens, and his hands become cold as stone. Steaming from within, fury begins to cook, begging to be unleashed.

Thus, he stands, puts out his cigar, and makes his way to the nearest exit. Meantime, Alma takes notice and proceeds to entertain the remaining audience of Diana's.

ABSTRACT

Officer Brian Brave Bronson is an influential police officer in Freeland City, glorified for his exceptional policing skills despite his thirst for whisky. His standing within Commissioner Sherman awards him the privilege of selecting his own uniform, reflecting the trust and significance placed in him. Notably, Brian has cultivated strong friendships with the likes of Susan Winters and Marcus Gibson, underscoring the persuasive network he has built.

EXTRA

Like Marcus, he, too, suffered a considerable loss. Brian's forefather perished in Freeland's Unrest, during which Michael Gibson participated that spanned across the entire city. His name was Brave Earl Bronson, formerly the Great Guardian.

WARRANT

Welcome to Freeland City, where fearless crime fighters rise to become legends, incredible crooks become infamous threats, and the clinically unhinged become dangerously unstoppable.
Become Wanted

A DYNAMIC PAIR

A DYNAMIC PAIR

Soon after the heroes' victorious efforts, brilliant headlights illuminate the lumber factory as the magnificent Oldsmobile arrives. Cutting the engine, a skilled subordinate circles the vehicle and reaches for the rear passenger door while *his* men await him.

"This way, sir."

Planting his sizable wingtips on the terrace, Astor exits the car and twists his neck to a loud crunch as he looks about. Reserved and suited for an event prior, he reaches into his coat for a spicy cigar, and with his crew, they proceed forward.

Passing the work area, smoke rivers from Astor's lips while his men guide him to Simon and his workers defeated.

"What happened here?" Counting his findings, Astor comes to recognize the hero's mark.

"I have failed you, Mr. Eckhard."

"I see."

"They've surely contacted the police."

BECOME WANTED: ACT TWO

Brooding at his failure to protect Astor's operation, Simon kneels before him to receive his outcome. Thus, Astor begins to imagine the crime fighter's newly discovered ally.

"They?"

#

Seeking higher ground, Marcus leads as Susan follows.

"How did you know that factory was a front for some bizarre crook's illegal weapons trade, huh?" Eyeing his car parked ahead, the soldier presses forward, hoping to lose the stubborn reporter.

"Let it rest, Susan."

"I know following you wasn't smart, but they had you back there, and if it weren't for me, you'd be up to your sunglasses with danger."

"You're way out of your element."

"Is that your plan…search for bad guys,

ruining their operations, so they can eventually catch up to you?

"How did you find me?"

"Well, your car is pretty noticeable," she teases.

"This isn't your fight, Susan," he claims as they reach the Shelby.

"You're right, it's not. But I can help you."

"With a tape recorder?"

"You could use a lookout." Reaching for the door, Marcus lingers, searching for a way to acknowledge her. "You're welcome," she pokes.

"That could have been the end for both of us back there."

"Well, we did good then, didn't we?"

"We? There is no we. Understand?"

"Wow, really? Interesting. For a moment back there, you were about to lose to those guys, and here you are, the hero of the evening. Yeah, thanks, Susan. You're welcome."

Bound by duty, Marcus realizes where he

may have misplaced his judgment. However, he remains unmoved and unable to share his next task with her.

"Do not follow me again." Entering his car, he starts the GTO, buckles up, and pulls away, vanishing into the night. As for the risky reporter, she simply reaches into her pocket to reveal her tape recorder still rolling and smiles.

"I'll see you again, detective."

Observing from the hill, the mystifying character who commands the fog manages to conceal his presence while a magnificent team carefully embarks on a dangerous journey, sharing one narrative that will truly be unforgettable.

"Well done, Marcus...well done."

THE COLLECTION

BECOME WANTED: ACT TWO

"More coffee, boys?"

Betty stood there, unsure of what to say. She can feel the tension between Marcus and Brian. So, she pours, for two, of course.

"You could at least take off the shades." She watches as Marcus refrains from acknowledging his friend policeman.

"It's bright in here." Eager to crack him, Brian presses the soldier again, but this time, he means it.

"Bright enough for a solid description." Avoiding the pressure, Marcus looks away. Yet, things done in the dark don't stay in the dark. "I've been by your father's place numerous times, and you weren't there, and now you show up with a fresh stitch over your brow," he points. "What the hell is going on?"

"So you're monitoring my whereabouts now?"

"Unless you can help me see otherwise?"

"Back off, Brian"

"Look...I just don't want to draw up a

report on you, that's all."

"Any new findings on my father's case?" he asks. "Because until I get some reassurance from you and Sherman, there's no telling what my whereabouts will lead."

Stunned, Brian falls back cushion while his friend curls over his almost-finished cup of coffee. Meanwhile, citizens in the diner tune in, including Betty.

"Sherman's leads have burnt out," he states. "The case will drown… and I'm not permitted to look into it."

"But I can."

"I had a feeling you'd say that."

#

Back at the police station, Commissioner Ronald P. Sherman summons Officer Brian Bronson for a status report on—

"Where's Marcus?" Inches away from his office, Brian slips in from the hallway just in time to catch Sherman putting out his cigar.

"He's well on his way, staying out of trouble just as you ordered, sir."

"Good. The last thing we need is Marcus toiling without agenda, agreed."

"Yes, sir," Brian confirms. Then—

RING, RING!

"Shit," Sherman grumbles.

RING, RING, RIIING!

"Let's move."

#

The GTO revs softly through the gates of Freeland City Police Memorial, passing grieving citizens leaving from a service that just passed. Remembering his last encounter with Susan after the Conductor's downfall, the war hero remains stony and steers forward.

Parked near his father's glorious monument, he steps out to find solace. He's prepared to engage more of Astor's henchmen to find his father's killer if necessary. Yet, he's missing one vital element.

"Will it stop, Marcus?" Suddenly, Susan joins him as the two look on to the sunset. "I'm afraid you're going to get yourself into something that only I can get you out of," she kids.

Defined yet, divided, he carefully turns to the bold reporter casting a hard ray with the edge of his forbearing sunglasses.

"Be alert, Susan, and I'll handle the rest."

Enduring alongside him, Susan resists the feeling of triumph while the brilliant colorings of the evening slowly vanish below the horizon.

#

"Our agendas have shifted, and as you all know, we've been hit." Valdemar, and The Collection, possessing powers beyond measure, convene unified at an expansive marble table at the epicenter of Vantous Tower. "I summoned you here for an announcement of great importance; new programs have been permitted to adjust the losses impacting your districts." Following his motions with their sights, seven unusual faces beside him depict the depths of Freeland's rising underworld. Nonetheless, he seeks to reclaim their trust with firm notions of effort and results, "In addition, impending expenditures on all assets will be waived until we can resolve this issue."

Evaluating his rapid proposal, they all nod in favor, all but one.

"And how do you plan to stop the crime fighter?"

"Julius: head of Howard Enterprises," he reveals, "Come again?" Stunned at his bid, although valid, the panel gradually expands, whereas Valdemar remains immersed in the topic.

"First Bruno, and then the Conductor... who's next?" Embracing the shadow behind him, the wicked director abandons his chair and starts down a path toward Julius.

"And every member at this table thrives nonetheless," he adds. Next, he shares a brief account of Michael Gibson that most but not all have failed to acknowledge. "Remember when the great detective of Freeland City was bent on exposing us?" Reaching the edge of the council, Valdemar conveys one last fact as he appears before Julius, "Where is he now?"

"Gone, yes. Though, here we are, on the verge of compromise due to Astor's unending blunders," he counters.

"Compromise?" Then, with the influence of a single hand, Julius tracks the director's motion to find a timid boy retained by two armed men near the entrance. "They found him shortly after the crime fighter's efforts. He has seen him with Skyland's Finest."

#

BECOME WANTED: ACT TWO

"Sir—you need to see this."

Sherman's oversized coat follows the heels of his shoes at the edge of a fresh crime scene, where Bronson joins him.

"Alright, enough with the games here… where is he?" Trembling with uncertainty, their coroner steps in to guide Sherman.

"Well, sir…he's *stuck* in there." Sapped with the situation, Sherman summons Brian to explore the foolish riddle.

"Release him." Locating an emergency panel, the clever cop pulls the reset button to free the contents of a great compactor.

SPLAT!

Coated in blood, Simon slips out from the chute in a grotesque shape of a cube shocking the entire team on the scene.

"SHIT!" Brian spews.

"This mill hasn't had an accident this horrid in Freeland history, Commissioner," claims the coroner.

"This was no accident."

DANNY STRIKES AGAIN

BECOME WANTED: ACT TWO

At the sunny start of the next day, the menacing trio enter Freeland Financial, the oldest bank institution in the city with a history dating back over 160 years.

The lobby is bustling with guests. Money is flowing, chatter is steady, and while the bank tellers are engaged at their stations, the bank guards at the entrance begin to shift warily; it was not long ago when Blue Dale's Bank was hit.

Suddenly, the air grows heavy with tension. A progression of knocks tapping against the marble floor gradually signals the return of danger. Then, with an eerie calmness, the odd men stop to address the customers of Freeland Financial.

"Good afternoon." The guests and staff immediately freeze in terror, witnessing the bank guards struggle uselessly in the arms of MARK-1 and MARK-2. Hence, the crook in all black proceeds, "My name is Danny Black, and I'm here to make a withdrawal,"

DANNY STRIKES AGAIN

he speaks. His peculiar accent and mild voice are equally menacing, and as he scans the lobby for particulars, he eventually identifies– "You—" The fearful vault keeper, scared beyond control, nods his head in resignation. "Do you carry gold here?"

Next, he pulls out his prized stopwatch, sets it for precisely ten minutes, and summons his minions to take the vault. As instructed, the two undead giants move in quickly, their black suits and fedoras a blur as they take out anyone who dares to stand in their way.

Meanwhile, Danny's eyes widen with satisfaction, for his plan is going precisely as intended.

#

Descending into the musical ironworks concealed beneath the city's notice, Dr. Noir prepares his hands for an intricate procedure.

"Now, observe closely, Toyface; the next

step is crucial. By the way…you can relax that boom-stick." Watching from afar, the silent assassin obeys his employer and cradles his weapon against his chest while remaining untouched by the gruesome mixture of bone, blood, and torn flesh encompassing the madman a mess. "The stiffening rate on this one is worse than the last," he remarks.

The oppressive darkness benefits the pair as the clamor of winding metal and sinister whispers fill the forsaken backdrop. The swinging lamp above them reveals glimpses of the horrors that lie within while the stench of decay and rust clings to their garments, skin, and even their lungs.

Observing in rooted silence, Toyface's sights enlarge with fascination, unable to tear his gaze from the dreadful scene unfolding before him. All the same, Dr. Noir's movements are deliberate and precise as he works feverishly with a bone saw to separate the top part from—

DANNY STRIKES AGAIN

CRUNCH!

Reaching up to steady the light, the cynical doctor finally beholds his masterpiece while his patient rests empty on the steel slab with their stony skin peeled back and pinned to their nose.

"Their minds are the key!" Flawlessly detached from the primary stem, he presents the victim's brain from its slimy home, only to find a defect almost instantly after its removal. "What is this?" he discovers. Examining the wrinkly organ intently, he makes no mistake in pointing out the rarest human flaw. "A tumor?" Timid not, the assassin stands unmoved. Yet, his chilling eyes follow the madman as he carefully sets the ruined item back into the patient's open skull. "Perhaps, we shall try again tomorrow."

Suddenly, on the small television box, Toyface loans his attention to the sound of Skyland's Finest, who appears with a tragic report. Meantime, Dr. Noir furthers to toil.

BECOME WANTED: ACT TWO

"Chaos erupted at Freeland Financial today as three masked assailants stormed the bank, leaving behind a trail of destruction. The ruthless crooks, dressed in tailored suits and black fedoras, carried out their heinous crime in broad daylight, causing numerous casualties led by Danny Black."

The sharp mention of the burglar and his two enforcers summons the doctor's concern as he turns in disbelief.

"While the search continues, we urge anyone with information that may lead to the capture of Danny to come forward."

"How did he do it?" Struck with intrigue, the madman returns to the lifeless patient, searching for an explanation for the impossible. "How do they walk, even after death?"

"As I attempt to bring this broadcast to a close, I can't help but wonder…where is our hero?"

#

DANNY STRIKES AGAIN

Glaring ahead from the back seat, Danny unwinds while his guardians steer him in the direction of their final destination; the gold is his, as marked in a significant carry-on kept beside him.

The heist has become the topic of discussion throughout Freeland, serving as a chilling reminder of the dangers that exist in the city. Despite Sherman and Bronson's best efforts, he and his undead monsters remain at liberty, with their true intentions and identities shrouded in mystery.

#

Bolting up the stairs, Marcus bursts into the study in search of information on Danny Black; he's hung up on Susan's story that terrified several in the city. His heart is pounding, time is ticking, and he must find anything on the mastermind and his immortal minions before they strike again.

THE GIFT OF LOVE

THE GIFT OF LOVE

Entering alone, Astor assumes a private elevator, enveloping him in an eerie silence as the steel doors close. The cab's walls are elegant and reflective, casting back distorted images of his face as he ascends higher and higher at Vantous Tower.

Reaching the twentieth floor, he steps out to find a dark hallway inviting him to take the extended way. The air is thick, as if the walls are closing in on him. However, he musters the courage to move forward.

Trudging down the forbidden corridor, his footsteps echo through the empty pathway, each step feeling heavier than the last. Finally, he finds the great doors, and with both hands, he pushes them open with all his might.

Upon entering, the space is vast and cold, with no trace of humanity or warmth to protect him. Thus, a sense of fear comes over him; he has failed *him* again.

The silence is deafening. The midnight speaks to Astor, taunting him, and as the brute aims to adjust to the darkness, the fabled Valdemar emerges from the shadows.

"The Collection is wary of your efforts, my son?" Determined to make amends for his shortcomings, Astor remains stoic, inviting him to pry. "Is something troubling you?"

Valdemar's penetrating gaze bores into him like a creature of the night stalking the weak, and being he is before Astor's time, he knows all.

"I punished Bruno and Simon with my bare hands, and when I catch the champion behind this, he will beg for the heavens," he replies. Suddenly, his father looms over him, for his true strength is undefined.

"Is that so?" His voice drips with scorn, and this angers Astor.

Still, determined not to cower in front of the founder of The Collection, he aims to persuade him further.

"I will find him and crush him like a cockroach beneath my shoe," he says.

THE GIFT OF LOVE

A glint of consent can be seen in his eyes, and a subtle grin follows.

"And that you shall, my son."

#

Fixed on the calm midnight through the passenger window, Astor remains in the back-seat of the Oldsmobile, pondering his father's final remarks; the tension between them still lingers with high importance.

Arriving at his residence, the brute takes a moment to admire the lush gardens, sparkling fountains, and imposing gates that protect him from outside forces. He is often reminded that his estate is not just a place to live; it symbol-izes his power and influence in the criminal underworld.

After exiting the vehicle, his most promis-ing men, armed with machine guns, approach him, pending their orders.

"Stay outside tonight."

BECOME WANTED: ACT TWO

The grandeur of the manor is accentuated by its southern-style architecture, embellished with an impressive arrangement of base lights that accentuate its grandeur. Standing tall at two stories, it is supported by a pair of bold pillars, adding to its colossal appeal.

Entering his home, an enchanting chandelier illuminates the grand beige interior, highlighting the many artworks encircling him and the marble flooring beneath his feet.

Climbing up a luxurious staircase, Astor takes in the brilliance of his abode. He has achieved success through force and strategic decision-making.

Reaching for the door handle, he reminds himself to appreciate the gift of love before he enters.

"I've been waiting for you." Reluctant to respond, he proceeds to a lavish class of gins, where he prepares two drinks: one for him and one for his lover, Alma. "I don't need another drink." The seductive singer turns to reveal to him her private body. "Let's leave Freeland—tonight." But to her surprise, her request fails to move him as he takes down his beverage in one deep swallow. She has challenged the gangster on many different levels regarding their deceptive relationship, but this matter is unlike before. She has stood by Astor through his darkest hours. But now, the situation has reached its limit, and so has she, "I'm leaving."

"That's enough, Alma," he voices. His comment silences the room, and yet, she is not ready to give up. She knows that he would do anything for her. However, the choice has already been made due to his involvement with Valdemar.

"He doesn't own you, Astor—he doesn't own us!"

"I said, that's enough!"

Deeply wounded, Alma abandons the window to hurl at Astor who, too, is upset.

"You fucking promised me," she cries.

BECOME WANTED: ACT TWO

Striving to restore her faith, he moves in to enfold her, drawing Alma near to calm her. Next, he aims to rest his hardened hands upon her trembling shoulders while guiding his lips towards hers in assuring unity.

"I will resolve this, my sweet angel…I just need more time," he declares, and as their passions spark into an uncontrollable blaze, he sweeps her onto his bed, an impressive piece crafted for royalty, where they abandon themselves to their sexual desires without limitation.

"Swear to me that we will leave Freeland soon," she pleads, longing for him to do what is necessary. Then again, the petrifying whispers of his father, Valdemar, quietly invades his thoughts. Hence, the brute chooses his following words carefully, minding the gravity they may carry.

"I swear it," he affirms. Yet the dread of discovery still lingers, casting a chilling shadow on their secret affair.

ASSAULT AT ASTOR'S ESTATE

BECOME WANTED: ACT TWO

Astor opens his eyes with a start. The deep lines in his face have never left, for his brutish nature never sleeps. His stiff yet vulnerable heart is pounding from a nightmare just before, and as he turns to his beloved Alma, lying peacefully beside him, he finds comfort in her presence.

But then, just as he begins to drift off to sleep—

RING, RII—

The shrill buzz of his telephone pierces the air, cutting through his moment of peace. Thus, he reaches over, and with a sense of panic lingering in his chest, he answers the call with a gruff,

"This'd better be good."

Outside, a mysterious detail wearing black-knitted masks and tactical jumpsuits swarm the mobster's property with a particular ideal in focus. Their identities remain a riddle. Furthermore, they're armed and determined as they advance across the grass, each step intensifying with every passing second.

Watching over Alma, the brute stands at the foot of his bed, tight with anticipation; the crime fighter has struck again. Stirring with anger, his thoughts commence to race, wondering how he can outwit the stubborn avenger. Understanding that failure is not an option, as his father said, Astor must act quickly in order to stay one step ahead of his nemesis.

Coming together in an execution-style formation, the invaders equip their weapons and stand by, awaiting command. The air surrounding them grows thick with uncertainty, and with their aims locked, they're finally given the order to open fire.

BOORAT-BOORAT-BOORAT!

High volumes of gunfire echo in the evening sky as bullets rip through the powerless estate. Fracturing the face of Astor's home, the firing team shift their fury to the top deck, aiming to destroy him where he rests.

BECOME WANTED: ACT TWO

Next, their commander appoints three shooters to infiltrate the shattered structure.

"Go." As ordered, they advance onward while he observes.

Once inside, they sweep the dining room, guest room, and the extensive living space where a luxurious piano is placed before proceeding up the stairs.

"Clear!" Casing the second story, they begin kicking in every entry preceding Astor's position with their barrels up. "Clear!" Each gunner is aware of the consequence of failure. Therefore, they're already dead.

Having cleared all areas aside from one, they briefly communicate, selecting one to enter Astor's private quarters while the others fall back for support.

CRACK!

Entering with a strong boot, the gunman unleashes a flare-up of gunfire, shredding everything in sight.

BOORAT-BOORAT-BOORAT!

ASSAULT AT ASTOR'S ESTATE

Lost in the sound of his weapon, he is unaware of Astor standing directly near him.

Enjoying a cigarette by the handrail, the second gunman turns sharply as the loose door slams shut and jams.

"What the fuck?"

Inside, the wary mercenary receives an unsuspecting push kick to the most vulnerable area of the back, thrusting him into a cabinet and glass mirror with disastrous impact.

"Who sent you?" Astor demands.

Listening to the cries from the outside, the second intruder hoists his weapon and, ultimately—

BOORAT-BOORAT-BOORAT!

Struck with disbelief, the shooter applies another magazine and, with undue caution, approaches the bullet-ridden entry.

"What the hell is going on up there?"

"Shut it, Fred; he's mine!" Bravely, he goes to inspect the shattered doorway when—

SMASH!

BECOME WANTED: ACT TWO

Astor breaks through, captures him, and pulls the intruder in.

"Barry! Are you clear up there?"

Dragging him through the door and to the floor, the brute flings the invader like a toy across the room to find his teammate broken by the cabinet.

"WHO SENT YOU?" Unlike before, he is furious beyond containment. Valdemar once spoke that Astor's savagery grants him the power to crush any man who defies him, and he was correct.

Refusing to speak, the devoted gunner climbs to his feet and launches his fist at the brute's square jaw.

CRUNCH!

Though, to his utter surprise, Astor's face remains intact, and as for his broken—

"Argh…my fucking hand!" he screams, shuddering at the sight of his twisted fingers. "You're gonna die!"

"Not before I make you suffer."

ASSAULT AT ASTOR'S ESTATE

Targeting Barry's torso, Astor launches into action, wrapping his arms around him, and with unforgiving might, he squeezes.

SNAP!

Watching the spirit flee from its shell, Astor begins to dig, but, to his dismay, he discovers something he had neglected from the beginning.

"You're a cop...how interesting."

Fred, the quivering and final gunman, as suggested by his shaky weapon, approaches the stairway when—

"YOU CAME INTO MY HOUSE!"

"Show yourself, Astor!" he shouts, and as the hunter becomes the hunted, Fred aims up to find two bodies soaring over the broad wooden banister, each crashing on the grand piano near him one by one.

PANG!

The sound of broken strings and clashing keys resounds throughout the living space, startling him entirely.

BECOME WANTED: ACT TWO

Standing in the stillness of the night, the commander waits vigilantly when his detail takes aim at the sight of activity happening at the entrance of the estate.

Marching through the busted walkway, Astor exposes their comrade, breathing and bleeding from a brutal beating.

"You won't be joining them," he whispers before casting Fred aside.

Seeing this, their leader instructs them to stand down, not before the sound of—

"Astor, please…stop."

The brute's wicked grin quickly reduces to find Alma behind him, clutching the handrail fixed to the stairs.

"Stay right there, my sweet angel; these men wouldn't dare." Inching to uncover their identities, he is fixed, bound between love and war, and as the event reaches its finale, the secretive player reveals a denoting mechanism before uttering these words.

"Goodbye, Mr. Eckhard."

ASSAULT AT ASTOR'S ESTATE

BEEP!

Suddenly, a powerful shockwave ripples throughout the entire estate. Bursts of fire erupt in various areas in his home. Minutes decrease to seconds allowing Astor to capture Alma only by sight—

"N-NOOO!"

KA-BOOM!

VIRGIL THE FALLEN

VIRGIL THE FALLEN

There are many channels hidden beneath Freeland, yet one lightless underpass befits a ghostly yet familiar character who commands the fog along his eerie course, and although the darkness has become his constant companion, the scurrying vermin underfoot serves as his guides down the narrow shaft.

"My name is Virgil the Fallen." Hinting at a haunting narrative of doom and demise, he suddenly halts on the tracks, overcome by a wrenching cough that pierces his hollow core. "Argh!" he grunts, "He took everything from me, and now…I am nothing more than a dying man under this hat and cape." Clinging to the fraying edges of Virgil's eternal cloak, a clever rodent escapes the clutches of the fog to find its place on his shoulder, silently urging him to persevere. "But how?" he asks. "How can I outwit a madman who eludes me at every turn…look at me?" His teeth, although intact, are exposed without lips to hide and a nose to remember.

BECOME WANTED: ACT TWO

Suddenly, a steel-grinding locomotive, whistling in the distance, fastly approaches at speeds far too dangerous for any traveler to be snagged in its path. Hence, its metal rattling urges the vermin to scatter, warning Virgil to do the same.

Hasten his steps, the watchful Inspector employs his walking cane to aid him, only to collapse due to his decline as the thunderous steam engine grows nearer.

CHUGGA-CHUGGA!

Weak and ravaged by wounds unhealed, the bold Inspector collects his cane, tucks his head and hat, and rolls off the rails to avoid the bypassing machine amid a death's touch.

CHOO-CHOO!

Escaping the treacherous tunnel, Virgil accesses a hidden path leading to a forgotten mechanical room devoid of its original machinery and control panels replaced by a collection of investigations; such a space of solitude has become his private study.

VIRGIL THE FALLEN

The room is dimly lit, with a single old lamp casting just enough light to illuminate his work area, where he spends much of his time. His desk and chair are equally weathered. Scattered documents, including cold case files, yellowed surveillance photographs, an age-old record player, and cryptic scribbles in his distinctive handwriting, reflect his tireless pursuit and withdrawn moments of introspection. Furthermore, the cracked walls surrounding Virgil serve as a haunting canvas for his rememberings exposed by newspaper clippings, showcasing both his past deeds and his devastating failures.

"I won't let you get away again…I can't afford to let you slip away for good." Scrolling over faded headlines portraying Freeland's misfortunes, including the death of Michael Gibson, a sudden flood of anger and sorrow takes over, transporting him back to a bygone era of his investigative career.

"It's all my fault."

ABSTRACT

Where the fog forms in Freeland, Inspector Virgil Lawson observes keenly, taking record of the city's ruthless wrongdoers and its daring heroes who have lost their lives defending it. Yet, among those whom the city mourns, the Inspector, too, bears injuries, and despite his limitations in physical strength and agility, he seeks help from those who can assist him in finishing what he started: to ruin crime and put an end to Dr. Noir.

EXTRA

Although suffering, Virgil is an exhaustive operative. During his laborious investigation beneath Freeland, he composed a confidential billfold containing evidence against the city's crooked underworld. However, having chosen Marcus to take action with the billfold's contents, he failed to hide one crucial detail from him.

WARRANT

Welcome to Freeland City, where fearless crime fighters rise to become legends, incredible crooks become infamous threats, and the clinically unhinged become dangerously unstoppable.
Become Wanted

LIMBO'S DECEPTION

LIMBO'S DECEPTION

Ensnared within the walls of Diana's, the ambiance was heavy with the smell of smoke and distorted laughter of the legless drunks and naked cocktail servers parading around like idiots on a stale night. Nevertheless, I pushed through, searching for the one person I was desperate to find. But, at last, I found her standing at the far end of the faded ballroom. Yet, her golden skin and wavy hair were unmistakable, and as I reached out to touch her, I realized with a crushing disappointment that it wasn't her.

"Get away from me," I said. But, from the lazy dame's gaze, she wasn't bothered, and they weren't paid to care, sadly.

Chips were thrown on the other side of the lounge, and appalling language was exchanged as hostility arose at the gambling table. Then the music stopped.

Quiet chatter expanded amongst the drunkards before they turned and pointed at me with their deceitful fingers, spewing hate out their filthy mouths.

"It's your fault she died…" Their voices annoyed me. How untrue…I would do anything for her.

"Anything?"

"Yes!" I shouted. "Haven't I shown that?" he begs. "I gave her money, fancy clothes, and a stage to showcase her talent—I own the very nightspot you judge me under!"

"You could have saved her…"

"No! They attempted to assassinate me, and she was stripped away from my grasp," and as frustration found me, sizzling cinders, descending from above, fell upon my face and hands, scorching me lightly. "What is this?" I asked, and when I looked up, I watched them vanish into ashes. My heart raced as I combed through the dead to find her, and as I dug and dug, an enormous spotlight unveiled the stage. So, I called out to her, "Alma!" I raced to the scene until I was close enough to touch her. "I thought I'd lost you." But as she began to burn and blister, the dead arose to hold me back from saving her. "Unhand me, ghouls." This couldn't be real. I fought through the dead and climbed onto the stage, yet I couldn't bear losing her again. "I have you…hang onto me," I cried, but as we touched, she finally fell into ashes in my arms.

#

"Alma…" Choking vapors instigated by black smog plug his lungs, spurring a fit of coughs that rip through his battered body. "ARGH!"

The agony is nearly unbearable. Pain, like a thousand needles, pricks at his every nerve, each bringing a new wave of torment. But when the thought of dying infests his mind, a jolt of desperation surges through him by way of the heart-wrenching scream of his beloved trapped within the inferno.

"ASTOR!"

BECOME WANTED: ACT TWO

"Alma?" he begs, a primal cry fueled by love and fear. Summoning every ounce of power gathered from within, he claws at the grass spot that holds him in the direction of the raging fire ahead. "A-ALMA!" Hindered by the searing pain in his legs, splinters of charred wood are embedded deep into his flesh, as he discovers in an attempt to rise. Determined to rescue the sole person to care for him outside his devotion to Valdemar, he continues to crawl through the scalding heat that scorches the last remnants of hope within him, but eventually and ultimately, the fire smothers her cries. "No...my sweet angel."

Tears of despair mixed with blood form in his aching eyes while the horrific finale reaches an end.

A growling sob flees his lips as the sound of crackling flames produces an insufferable spiral of misery as it continues to devour Alma Arcos mercilessly before him. Hence, and hereby, he has lost her forever.

LIMBO'S DECEPTION

As the fire glows on, the agony of Astor's loss burrows deeper and deeper, searing into his very soul. In this moment of devastation, he is simultaneously beaten by the physical pain of his injuries and the crushing weight of his emotional grief.

SUSAN'S PEACE & A FIERY END

SUSAN'S PEACE & A FIERY END

Returning to her studio located sixteen blocks from the news station, Susan keys the lock quickly and enters, closing the door behind with the weight of Freeland's current circumstances. Overwhelmed by the horrific event involving Danny Black and his sinister, automated-like guardians, she tosses her keys onto the table by the entrance and strides toward her bedroom, with each step exuding a mixture of anxiety and frustration, weighing her down all the same.

Her home is sparsely furnished with a typewriter and worktop, a nifty camera for spying purposes, and a disguise, all tools of her trade. On the walls are maps and underground layouts of Freeland, annotated with her findings, along with shelves lined with notebooks crammed with details from past interviews and pending investigations.

Susan has been a reporter for Skyland for more than a decade, and her studio reflects her long-standing career shown in various

BECOME WANTED: ACT TWO

articles, awards, and a degree in Journalism.

Peeling off the clothing that clings to her like a constant reminder of the day's ordeal, she endures the struggle with a storm of emotions swirling beneath the surface.

With a sigh of relief, Susan tilts her head back, allowing the water to pour over her soft edges. The clear beads dripping from her body catch the light, creating a mesmerizing dance of liquid diamonds. She takes a deep breath, inhaling the steam that swirls around her, creating a protective cocoon that shields her from the outside world.

For a precious moment, Susan's world is reduced to the sound of water, the warmth of the steam, and the gentle touch of the droplets on her skin. Her worries dissolve, carried away by the currents flowing down the drain. But just as she begins to fully surrender to this calming oasis, a shrieking rattle pierces the tranquility.

RING, RING, RING!

SUSAN'S PEACE & A FIERY END

The shrilling sound pulls her back to reality, splitting her sanctuary of serenity. Reluctantly, Susan cuts the water, snatches a towel, and bolts for the phone, ready to face the world once more.

RING, RII—

"Talk to me."

#

Engulfing Astor Eckhard's estate, voracious flames dance wildly against the night sky, casting a ghostly glow on the surrounding province.

Firefighters, swarming the site, battle the relentless blaze with their hoses, unleashing torrents of water in a desperate attempt to tame the inferno.

Amidst the tireless sound of sirens and crackling embers, Commissioner Sherman, as seen in his favorite overcoat and polished badge pinned to his lapel, stands stoically at the heart of the sprawling crime scene, scanning the fiery pandemonium with an attitude of composed detachment.

As the night wears on, he fishes a cigar out of his trench coat pocket. Judging from its width, length, and dark and lustrous appeal, most would agree that he favors the kind that burns slowly with a bitter bite. Given a strike of his bronze lighter, he torches it and clamps it firmly between his teeth, allowing the aromatic smoke to mingle with the dense smog of the once-magnificent burning property.

As the tenacious medical examiners, clad in white protective suits, hoist several body bags onto stretchers, Sherman finally raises a commanding hand to flag them down.

"Hold on there."

"Yes, sir."

Selecting one at random, he gazes at it intently before unzipping its contents to unveil a wisp of smoke and the overpowering stench of charred flesh.

SUSAN'S PEACE & A FIERY END

Yet, he remains cold as he notes a distinctive earring still attached to the corpse's left ear.

"Goddamn it, Ms. Arcos."

Lastly, with a curt nod, he gestures for the medical men to move on, leaving him to piece together the complex puzzle of this devastating disaster.

ABSTRACT

Fixed on uncovering the untried, Skyland's Finest-Susan Winters is Freeland's appointed anchor and news journalist. Widely celebrated for her mastery of storytelling within the world of local news, Susan's remarkable efforts to expose the hidden agendas that lurk beneath the city have earned her the esteem and confidence of viewers throughout her community.

EXTRA

Moved by her continued curiosity for conspiracies, Susan has sought out several interviews and secured many, but the frightening myth surrounding the methodical madman Dr. Noir fascinates her, and perhaps for deeply personal reasons.

WARRANT

Welcome to Freeland City, where fearless crime fighters rise to become legends, incredible crooks become infamous threats, and the clinically unhinged become dangerously unstoppable.
Become Wanted

ASTOR REBORN

ASTOR REBORN

Heavy rain plummets over "Phillip's and Son's," turning the large terrace to muck. Since Marcus defeated Simon, the decaying structure had been taped off from the public. Trudging through the muddy grounds, a significant character disguised under a hooded rain cape pushes through the downpour seeking refuge.

The drifter eventually reaches the factory's front entrance to find the massive gate fortified by lock and chain; however, mere metal stands no contest to a desperate man. Thus, he grabs ahold of the iron links and, with great might, wrenches them away.

Once inside, he bears a moment to scan the empty mill to uncover multiple footprints left by the law during their raid, visible in the sticky sawdust plastered on the ground. Passing through the condemned factory, the weeping crook finds a solid sledgehammer, snares the large, two-headed mallet, and continues through the abandoned facility.

BECOME WANTED: ACT TWO

Standing where the high-powered crime fighter held his battle against the Conductor, he locates an area left untouched during the police's conclusive investigation.

His father made brief warnings before his utter downfall, yet here he is. The shattered racketeer approaches a large stack of oil drums and kicks them down to reveal a conspicuously bare area, distinctly discolored compared to the main operating floor.

Fueled by his tragic loss and past failures, he embraces the iron hammer, hoists it up high above his head, and brings it down to the ground with every ounce of pain.

CRACK! CRACK! CRACK!

Over and over again, he pounds the deck, piercing the concrete until ruined.

SMASH!

Severely drained, he tosses the hammer only to fall to his aching knees in desolation. There, he removes his cape, revealing himself as none other than Astor Eckhard.

ASTOR REBORN

"I will avenge you," he declares. Yet, his tears that fall gradually turn to wrath, urging him to scrape away the loose cement with his worn hands. "I will make them pay." Digging until he can no longer, he reaches into the gaping hole to haul out a worn duffle bag and unzips it to recover his memorable sub-machine gun. "I will find them, and when I do," Rejoined with his weapon of war, a sudden thunder strike claps in the distance, forecasting destruction, to be exact, "I will stretch them apart limb by limb."

To Be Continued...

BECOMING WANTED

BECOME WANTED: ACT TWO

My journey as an author in this wonderful world of literature has been incredible. Crafting stories and interesting characters that come to life in our reads has become my dream. Thus, casting real talent to portray our heroes and wrongdoers became what I am known for today.

This particular story is very special, for it is because of *Become Wanted* that I became a writer.

The satisfaction that comes from piecing together actions and sequences to generate an entertaining and captivating narrative is indescribable to say the least.

Moreover, I am proud of my work and my team, and together, we have created some interesting fictions that will remain in our hearts and hopefully yours for many years to come.

David

A HERO IN DANGER

A HERO IN DANGER

Beyond Central Freeland's innermost city limits, Marcus arrives at a downbeat location in his stylish GTO. While the car hums, he retrieves a crumpled file from his coat pocket and gently cuts the engine. The air is bitter with a serious chemical, causing his nose to wrinkle. Coming across the only means of access, he senses something is amiss, yet the coordinates in the confidential report lead him here.

Climbing down to a cold passageway, the clang of iron bars and the smell of sweat and desperation forewarns him to stay alert. The uncertainty of his pursuit only strengthens his resolve to uncover this criminal operation. Unafraid, he moves forward.

As he moves further into the facility, he discovers a line of iron cells, each one containing a girl with a story to tell and a cry for help. Still, Marcus quickly puts together an effort while taking in the reality of the situation.

BECOME WANTED: ACT TWO

"I'm here to free you, Alice," he whispers. As he scans the iron frame to her cell, she looks up to see the generous war hero she had met some time ago.

"Hey...you're the brave man who beat up Bulldog, huh?" she recalls.

"You got that right," he confirms.

Suddenly, racing footsteps approaching Marcus from behind frighten the girl from Harlots, and before he can act, the crime-fighter receives a cheap blow to the back of his head.

BAM!

Moments later, Skyland's Finest arrives at the shared location and spots the spotless Shelby parked. All the same, she senses a strange suspicion and prepares to enter the already-discovered entrance.

"Be alert, he said." Her heart races as she activates her tape recorder and steps further into the facility. Meanwhile, Susan's entry doesn't go unnoticed.

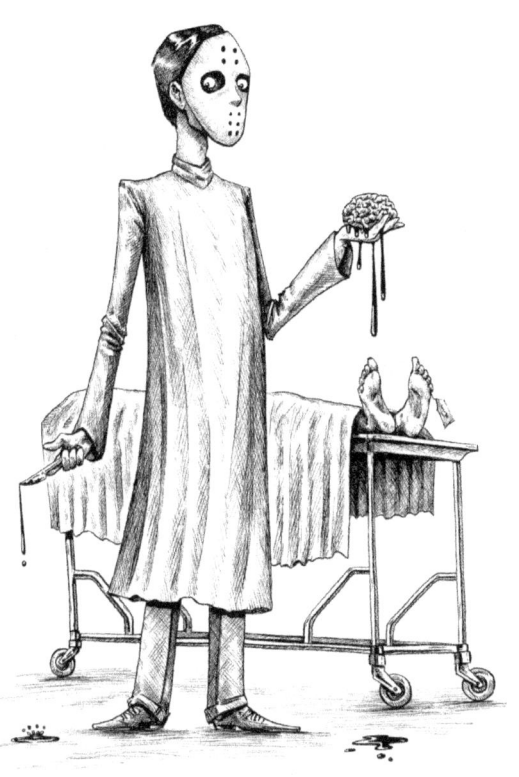

www.becomewanted.com